Hello Kayden

I found this book recently and thought you might enjoy it.

Love
Grandma
Nancy

Pig and Bear

Vít Hořejš

Pig and Bear

ILLUSTRATED BY
Friso Henstra

FOUR WINDS PRESS

NEW YORK

Four Winds Press, Macmillan Publishing Company, 866 Third Avenue, New York, NY 10022.
Collier Macmillan Canada, Inc.

First Edition   Printed in the United States of America   10   9   8   7   6   5   4   3   2   1

The text of this book is set in 13 point Galliard. The illustrations are rendered in pen-and-ink.

Library of Congress Cataloging-in-Publication Data
Hořejš, Vít. Pig and Bear/Vít Hořejš; illustrated by Friso Henstra. — 1st ed.   p.   cm.
Summary: Pig and Bear's friendship survives several amusing misunderstandings.
ISBN 0-02-744421-X
[1. Pigs—Fiction. 2. Bears—Fiction. 3. Friendship—Fiction.] I. Henstra, Friso, ill. II. Title
PZ7.H7808Pi 1989   [E]—dc 19   88-21304   CIP   AC

TO

BONNIE

SUE

STEIN

CONTENTS

CHAPTER ONE   How Pig and Bear
                Opened a Pawnshop   I

CHAPTER TWO   Pig and Bear in Danger,
                Very Little Beings, and
                Their Mysterious Changes   8

CHAPTER THREE   Which Should Be about
                Pig and Bear at the Movies
                but Turns Out Otherwise   19

CHAPTER FOUR   How Pig and Bear
                Got Telephones   28

How Pig and Bear
Opened a Pawnshop

Pig and Bear had their own cottages, each one in a different part of the forest. The cottages were not so very far away from each other, but not so close either. All the same, the two friends spent most of their time together. For some reason, Bear slept mostly in Pig's cottage, but Pig stayed over at Bear's quite often, too. Sometimes they planned their visits that way, and sometimes they decided what to do on the spur of the moment. But most of the time they just fell asleep on the spot before they could plan or decide anything.

"Let's open a pawnshop," Pig said while visiting at Bear's one sunny afternoon.

"All right," said Bear, who was sitting in his favorite rocker, thinking. He opened one eye and added, "It's a wonderful idea."

A week went by. The next Tuesday, at the stroke of noon, there was a knock on Pig's door.

Pig turned over on his left ear, but the knocking wouldn't go away. He stuck on his slippers and shuffled to the door. He opened it, but no one was there.

Pig was about to go back to bed when he heard snoring. The sound came from a pile of fur on his porch. He poked the fur with his thumb and jumped back as it growled fiercely.

Then the fur said in Bear's voice, "Why are you waking me up so early?"

"Who? Where? You woke *me* up," said Pig. "Didn't you just knock at my door? You nearly knocked my house down!"

"Oh, did I?"

"You did."

"I might have," murmured Bear. "But that's no reason to wake me up. So early in the morning."

"But you just . . ."

"Oh, yes, I remember! I . . . I knocked and knocked, and nobody answered. Did you just come home?"

"Just why *did* you wake me up?" Pig asked sharply.

"Why . . . why . . ." Bear mumbled. "Oh, I know, I know! We decided to open a *pawshop*. I woke up at eleven o'clock, and the sun was already up and shining. This is the day, I thought, to open a *pawshop*. So I came to get you."

"Of course this is the best day," said Pig. "I've been getting ready since dawn. Where should the *pawnshop* be?" he asked his friend.

"I don't know." Bear scratched his shoulder.

"Well!" Pig said importantly. He crossed over to the hammock and stretched out in it. "Not only did you sleep until eleven, you don't even know where the *pawnshop* will be. And on the day we're supposed to open it!"

"I don't really know *what* a *pawshop* is." Bear twisted his body, trying to scratch in the middle of his back this time.

There was a silence.

"I know I should know," Bear said finally. "I used to. Can you tell me? Please?"

"Well, how can I explain it. . . . It's something that . . . A *pawnshop* is . . . It's funny, I can't remember right now. Whose idea was it, anyway?"

Bear sighed. "I am afraid it was ours."

"Hm," they said together.

"Let's think," said Pig.

They thought. They thought. They looked at each other. They looked at the sky. They thought some more.

"Oh!" said Pig. "The *pawnbroker*."

"The what?"

"The *pawnbroker* works in the *pawnshop*."

"Now I remember," said Bear. "What does he do?"

"Makes lots of money."

"Right! Right! We wanted to open a *pawshop* to make lots of money!"

"That's it!"

There was another silence.

"I don't think I want to do that," Bear said sadly.

"Why not?"

"I don't think a *pawbroker* only makes money."

"What else does a *pawnbroker* do?"

"*Breaks paws.*"

"Does he?"

"I think so."

There was a *long* silence. Pig kept opening and closing his snout and making little squealing sounds as if he were going to speak.

Finally Bear said slowly, "I thought maybe . . . maybe a

pawshop was a place where animals went when they didn't feel so good . . . and a big warm paw patted them. Or just held them. Tight."

"Oh." Pig rolled out of the hammock. "I like that. Let's do *that*."

"But what about the *pawbroker*?" Bear asked anxiously.

"Nothing!" said Pig, getting up and dusting himself off. "We'll have nothing to do with *pawnbrokers* . . . I mean, *pawbrokers*." He stopped with a gaping snort. "It's an entirely different word," he finally blurted, startling Bear, who was climbing into the empty hammock. "You mixed me up. A *pawnbroker* doesn't have anything to do with *pawshops*. The *pawnbroker* works in a *pawnshop*. Two entirely different, closely related words."

"But what about . . . " Bear began dreamily.

"Nothing. No pawbreaking and no big warm paw. Oh, that's really too bad, isn't it? It felt *so good* to think about such a big warm paw."

"Zzzzzz," answered Bear, who had fallen asleep on the sunny porch.

Pig grunted. "How can you sleep at a time like this?" He climbed back into the hammock to wake up his friend. Then he began to feel really comfortable, and soon he, too, fell asleep in the warm sun.

6

Bear slept on his left side, and Pig slept on his right side next to Bear. After a bit, Pig opened his eyes. He saw that Bear's eyes were wide open, too.

This is our *pawshop*, Pig wanted to say. But he saw in Bear's eyes that Bear knew, so he didn't say anything. They both went to sleep again, Pig's hoof tight in Bear's paw.

CHAPTER TWO

Pig and Bear in Danger, Very Little Beings, and Their Mysterious Changes

Close the door, fast," Pig squealed as Bear entered his cottage one Sunday afternoon. "Don't let *them* in with you."

Bear didn't usually bother closing doors, but he was alarmed by Pig's words. He slammed the door and held it tight.

There was no banging on the door. No one tried as much as to turn the doorknob.

"Seems I had a narrow escape!" Bear's eyes darted from side to side. "Are we in *danger*?" he whispered.

"Relax," said Pig, who was crouching by the window. "I told you to close the door only because I didn't want the *outsects* to get in."

"The *outsects*?" Bear leaned against the door with more force.

"They're bad enough to deal with in the forest," Pig said. "I don't want them inside."

Bear was holding the door with all his might. "Do you think these *outsects* could force the door open?" he asked, panting.

"Of course not," Pig said. "They are *very little beings*. But I think there is a chink under the window here where they can creep in. Then they change. They are much fiercer after they change."

"Do they become real big?"

"I wonder when, exactly, they change?" Pig asked himself, ignoring Bear's question. "It's pretty clear when they change if they come through the door, but I really don't know about the chink."

"You mean these *outsects* become very small when they crawl in"—there was sweat on Bear's brow—"and then they become big and fierce inside?"

"Nonsense," Pig said casually. "They're always small, only they are not *outsects* anymore once they get in."

"I think I'll be going," Bear said. "It was very nice seeing you."

"Just close the door behind you tight," Pig said. He crimped himself up and twisted his neck remarkably. Trying to look deeper into the chink under the window, he almost squeezed his eye inside. "One or two can be taken care of easily, but I don't want them to *swarm in*. Did you leave your door closed when you left your house?"

"Oh," Bear said. "Let me think. . . . I think I won't be going after all."

"Nice of you," Pig said absentmindedly.

"Do you think," Bear said in a thin voice, "do you think that if somebody, some very friendly animal that doesn't do any harm to anybody, if he left his door open, do you think the *outsects* would be there, waiting for him? Do you think they would be *disposed* against him in some way?"

"Definitely," Pig said sadly. "I mean, as I said, once they get in, they are not *outsects* anymore. They become *insects*. Very fierce and buzzy, with no regard whatsoever."

"Oh."

"I've been studying them for quite a while," Pig said. "I tried the slapping test, the pillow-fighting test, and playing dead, but all with the same result. A mosquito *inside* a room, for instance, is much fiercer and treacherouser than he can ever be *outside*. Now, it is very important to find out exactly when an outsect becomes an insect. I am deeply convinced that at this *in-between moment*, the very small beings are harmless, while it is hard to catch an outsect and almost impossible to outsmart an insect."

The scientific problem took over Bear's mind. "What if you swallow an outsect?" he asked.

"Very unpleasant, happens quite often," said Pig. "Makes you cough. Face reddens, eyes fill with tears. Not very tasty, either."

"I mean, does he become an insect?"

"Very interesting question." Pig clacked his tongue. He began to pace the homespun rug in front of his bookcase. Then he climbed on a small stepladder and reached to the top shelf to pull the biggest book out. (It was the biggest of the only two books. The rest of the bookcase was stuffed with seashells, pinecones, acorns, chestnuts, twisted roots, interesting rocks, and other useful things.)

"Let me show you." Pig leafed through the dog-eared encyclopedia in his lap. "Here!"

Bear leaned forward eagerly. His friend put his hooves over the color illustration. "Of course, there are two schools of thought," Pig went on. "One part of me maintains that a swallowed outsect cannot change into an insect anymore. But the other part of me, mainly hind legs, back, and kidneys, is of the opinion that the outsects change into insects, dead or alive." With these words Pig slapped the book closed and put it back on the shelf.

"What about a fly in the eye?" Bear asked after a pause.

"Definitely."

"Definitely what?"

"An insect. A very fierce one."

"What about ants in my fur?"

"Think about it," Pig said, climbing down from the stepladder. "Do the ants outside your fur seem fierce?"

"Mmhhm . . . " Bear scratched the back of his head. "If I think about their *getting* in my fur, they seem extremely fierce."

"That's because you are imagining them as insects while they are still outsects."

"And the stinkbugs?" Bear wrinkled his nose.

"In your fur?"

"No, anywhere. On blueberries. They are very fierce at making blueberries stink."

"A fierce outsect."

For a while they pondered the fierceness of stinkbugs. Then Bear asked, "What about a ladybug?"

"On a blueberry?"

"In my paw?"

"Well . . . she's an outsect as long as your paw is opened. When you close it, she becomes an insect . . . a very gentle one."

"It tickles." Bear gave a little laugh.

"Of course it does. Very gently."

"No, I mean, yes, but it tickles now. Something is crawling up my leg."

Pig looked closely at his friend. A strange insect—or was it an outsect?—was making its way up Bear's right calf. It had several pairs of legs on its beginning and on its end. It raised its front legs, pushed them forward, arched its body, and stepped with its hind legs close to its head. Looping around in this way, the insect tickled its way to Bear's knee.

Pig and Bear stared.

"It is an inchworm," Pig said finally. "Let me show you." He climbed up on the ladder again and reached for the book but didn't pull it down. "You are going to get a new suit," he said. "The inchworm is taking your measurements."

"Really?" For some reason Bear was whispering. "How do you know?"

"My grandmother always said so, when an inchworm walked over me or my brothers."

"Oh, really! I've never had a suit. I always wear my fur coat. Do you think I'll have to wear a tie?"

"Me and my brothers always had to." Pig climbed down from the stepladder.

The inchworm was now tickling past Bear's knee. It seemed to hesitate there, with its head and front legs raised, moving from side to side.

"Do you think he's choosing the fabric?" Bear whispered. "Do you think I could talk to him about the color?"

They watched the inchworm take all measurements: inseam, waist, chest, sleeve length, cuffs, and collar.

Bear held his breath so hard that he went to sleep.

Pig was guarding Bear's sleep for at least five minutes before he went to sleep, too.

Bear dreamed about ladybugs crawling through the chink under the window. They tickled. Pig also dreamed something about a very gentle outsect changing into an insect and putting on a new suit that tickled. But Pig could never remember dreams clearly, and he had forgotten this one completely when he woke up an hour later. He had even forgotten where he was. As soon as he figured out it was his own cottage, Pig shook his friend's arm. "Wake up. Your tailor wants to leave."

"What, where, who?" Bear asked brilliantly.

"We have to let the inchworm out." Pig pulled on Bear's arm again. "He's measured you three times now. He's going to make you a hat and earmuffs. Right now he's taking the measure for a nose guard. Don't sneeze!"

Pig led his friend to the door, opened it carefully just a tiny bit, and whispered, "Watch out, we don't want any unfriendly outsects to get in!"

Bear squeezed his nose into the gap to let the inchworm loop his way out.

"Dob't close it byet," he said anxiously, as he felt the door squeezing his nose. Then he pulled back.

Pig closed the door fast. "Did you see?"

"Yes, I bdid." Bear touched his nose gently with his paw. "Id's dbeautiful. Led's go out."

"I mean, did you see any outsects?"

"I saw some beautiful *outterflies*. Let's go and see them."

They opened the door slowly, ready to slam it against any unfriendly outsects. None were in sight. Only the colorful butterflies flittered above blooming flowers. A cricket orchestra was rehearsing somewhere in the grass, and a pair of dragonflies with polished wings buzzed in a low flight over the porch. Holding onto each other, just in case, Pig and Bear walked bravely back into the world of outsects.

A polka-dotted butterfly danced in the hot air.

"There's a bowtie for you," Pig said.

As they followed it onto the path, the butterfly swooped toward them and circled Bear as if looking for a place to land, but then it flew away. Perhaps it decided to wait until Bear's new suit was finished.

CHAPTER THREE

Which Should Be about Pig and Bear at the Movies but Turns Out Otherwise

I think I am going to the movies today," Bear said one Saturday afternoon. He told his plan to the big clock in Pig's living room.

"That's a great idea," Pig squealed. "But it's such a sunny day, maybe we should go and pick some acorns."

"All right," Bear agreed without much excitement. "Let's."

"Or pinecones," Pig said, changing his mind.

"Picking pinecones is just pfine," Bear mumbled sadly.

Pig sighed. "I wish that you would *fight* sometimes for what you really think," he told Bear. "That you wouldn't just nod and grunt like you agree when you're not quite sure about it."

"I never fight," Bear said. "You may like fighting, but I—"

"Look who's fighting!" Pig snorted lightly.

"I am not!" Although he didn't mean to, Bear sounded a bit crabby. "Stop picking on me!"

"You are, you are . . . *contradicting* me. You always do."

"I never contradict anybody!" Bear insisted with a little growl. "That includes you."

"Don't growl at me." Pig lifted his snout toward the ceiling.

"I only growled because you were trying to convince me that I was fighting you, but I wasn't. I never fight. *You* fight."

"Look who's talking!"

"Don't say 'Look who's talking!' to me!" Bear said.

"Stop ordering me around!" snapped Pig.

"I am not ordering you around!"

"Now you're *contradicting* me again! Can't I ever be right?"

"I . . . am . . . not . . . fighting!!!" Bear roared so loudly that the windows shook.

"Okay, okay, you're not fighting. You never fight. I am the only one. Sorry I made you yell and growl and roar at me. It's all my fault."

"I—"

"No, no, no, no. Please, don't say anything! Let's forget it. I might make you growl and roar at me again, and someone might hear it and think that you're fighting, but you never fight so—"

"I am sorry I growled, but—" Bear began, but Pig interrupted him.

"No, no, no—it's all my fault. Just growl and roar at me whenever you feel like it, as long as it makes you feel that you're right and that you're not fighting."

"I am not!"

"Whatever you say."

There was a long pause. Bear paced back and forth on Pig's rug. He looked rather nervous.

"I wonder if it's going to rain tomorrow," Pig said.

"Huh?" Bear jerked his head toward Pig.

"Maybe it won't," Pig answered himself.

"Maybe."

"Or just a little."

"I wish"—Bear squeezed the words out of his throat with effort—"I wish that you could really understand that I don't want to quarrel."

"But sure—"

"I wish you wouldn't just talk about rain or snow or tornadoes when we are having—when we are *not having* a fight."

"Listen," Pig said sweetly, "there's nothing we can really fight about because I believe whatever you say. Now, do you think it's going to rain tomorrow?"

"No!!!! There's going to be an earthquake!"

"Whatever you say."

"Say that one more time," Bear rasped slowly, "and I'll never talk to you again."

"I can say whatever I please, because I am being polite, you . . . overbearing bear. You've been ordering me around enough. *I* will never talk to *you* again!"

Bear's muzzle slowly became red under his fur. Then he turned around, stormed out the door, and slammed it behind him. Above the door, a framed portrait of Pig's grandfather swayed on its hook.

Thump, thump, thump, resounded Bear's steps on the porch. Then Pig heard a *bang* followed by an "Ouch!" and a dull *bump, bump.*

For a long while, there was a complete silence. Then the framed portrait over the door finally made up its mind and crashed to the floor. Pig, who had seemed frozen where he stood, gave a start and ran out the door.

Bear had already picked himself up from the path. When Pig saw this, he stopped so suddenly that he had to catch his balance on the porch railing. After several moments of uncertainty as to whether he, too, would go *bump, bump* off the porch, he composed himself and began pacing back and forth, watching the clouds. He made it as clear as possible that he had run out of his cottage for that purpose only.

Bear's mind was taken away from his own mishap by Pig's balancing act. Finally he closed his mouth and took a step toward Pig, but then he turned about and walked toward the forest, mumbling into his whiskers.

When he turned around at the edge of the trees, he saw that Pig had found out the clouds needed watching from quite far down the path. Bear decided to walk casually back and forth between the forest and Pig's porch.

Pig decided to walk back and forth, too. Soon he noticed that Bear was much closer than before. He spun about fast and walked back to the porch. At their next turn, Pig was only about twenty-six steps behind Bear, and, at the next, Bear was only eight and a half steps behind Pig.

The next time Pig reached the porch, they made the turn together and walked, side by side, to the forest and back. When they finally started speaking, they did it both at the same time, and then stopped again.

"I am sorry," said Bear.

"Oh, no, go ahead. You spoke first." Pig shook his head.

"I mean, I am sorry for all that happened before."

"That's all right, I . . . I wasn't very nice to you."

"No, it's all my fault."

"I was picking on you. . . ."

"I was fighting with you. . . ."

"It's all right," they said, speaking both at the same time again. In silence they made another trip to the forest and back.

"I was afraid," Bear said. "I was afraid that you . . . that we would never be friends again."

"And I thought that you would walk into that forest and I would never see you again in my life," Pig said in a soft voice.

"As I was walking away from your cottage it seemed the longest five minutes in my life."

"When you turned and hesitated, I was sure you wouldn't come back."

They made about thirty trips back and forth between Pig's cottage and the forest. Then Pig walked Bear home, and Bear walked Pig back again. By that time Pig was really tired, but he walked Bear halfway back. They parted in the middle of the forest, shook paws and hooves, and squeezed them hard.

"I promise I'll never fight again," Pig said. "Except sometimes."

"And I won't either, I promise," Bear said. "Except maybe sometimes," he added quickly, "when you want me to."

CHAPTER FOUR

How Pig and Bear
Got Telephones

One sunny morning Pig and Bear woke up in Pig's cottage just in time for a small lunch. They ate Pig's favorite: cereal topped with honey, raisins, almonds, cashew nuts, Brazil nuts, hazelnuts, pecans, hickory nuts, pumpkin seeds, sesame seeds, sunflower seeds, figs, dried apricots, papaya, and pineapple. Then they had some potatoes, cauliflower, and fresh carrots; a little salad on the side with lots of blue-cheese dressing; some chocolate-walnut cake; and a small dish of butterscotch ice cream, followed by a second one, just a bit bigger, and then a really big one to finish.

That morning Pig said, "What would you do if you needed to get hold of me fast?"

"I'd grab ya." Bear proceeded to show what he meant.

Pig jerked out of the reach of Bear's paws and said quickly, "I mean, what would you do if you wanted to get a short urgent message to me?"

Bear was quite used to sudden, unexpected questions from Pig. He answered without too much thought. "If it were a *really* short message, I'd just give it to you. If it were a medium-long short message, you'd most likely interrupt me before—"

"But *how* would you give it to me?" said Pig.

"What do you mean? I'd tell it to you."

"How would you tell me if you were in your cottage?"

"The same way as here." Bear spread out his paws. "I give short urgent messages the same way, no matter where I am."

"If you were in your cottage and I were here, I mean!"

"I guess I'd walk over."

"But if it were a *really urgent short message*!" Pig insisted.

"I'd walk fast. Perhaps, if I knew the day before that I would want to give you a short urgent message the day after, I'd just stay over to be here to tell you."

Pig sighed and rolled his small eyes. "You don't know about short urgent messages. They are given in *emergencies*. The way you talk, you've probably never been in an emergency or given a short urgent message in your life. I'll have to explain to you later how to get into an emergency. But let me tell you about the idea I just had for giving short urgent messages. It's called a *telephone*."

"Mmhhm . . . I don't know about *using* a *telephant* for anything. I think a *telephant* gives basically one short urgent message, which is to get out of the way of its long trunk."

"A *telephone*, not a *telephant*. A telephone like the frogs have."

"Well, I know the frogs think everything they have to croak is highly important and urgent," said Bear. "They can hardly ever stop croaking, whether on the *telephont* or not. Was a *telephont* really your idea?"

"It was my idea as far as passing short urgent messages between the two of us is concerned," Pig said. "You see, I got a letter from the Tinkerbell Company last week, and it gave me the idea. Because they are installing them for nearly nothing and they charge only 7.2 cents for a short call. So I suddenly had this idea that we should have telephones in our cottages in case of any emergency. I mean, even if I teach you how to get into emergencies, the phone calls won't cost us too much, because emergencies are *rare*."

Bear thought about it. Four days later a crew of cranes from the Tinkerbell Company strung wires between their cottages and installed telephones in them. It cost a little more than the letter from the Tinkerbell Company had said, but the telephones were beautiful—shiny and sleek.

It so happened, however, that in the next two weeks Pig and Bear stayed together all the time and didn't use the phones at all. Finally Pig said Bear had to go home, because otherwise they could miss some emergency and the opportunity of giving each other a short urgent message.

Bear considered saying something about an emergency's being more important to Pig than he, Bear, was. But then he decided Pig was right and walked home to his cottage. As usual, he took the shortcut.

The forest path was balmy and fragrant. Bear walked at a comfortable pace, singing,

"El-ergency, em-ergency,
Youppity, youppity, yooo

En-ergency, o-pergency,
Brave Bear is ready for you

Cue-ergency, arr-ergency . . .”

And so on. Nearing his cottage, he heard a clear ringing sound. He ran the last fifty paces, bolted through the door, and grabbed the telephone.

"Bear speaking!" he gasped.

"Pig speaking!" squealed the earphone. "Where have you been? I've been calling for hours!"

"What happened?" Bear was still catching his breath.

"Nothing. What should have happened?"

"What is the short urgent message, I mean?"

"Nothing."

"You mean, you're calling without an emergency?"

"And I am sure lucky there wasn't any. I just wanted to check if you were there so that I could start looking for one. How's the weather?"

"Looks fine. Rather hot." Bear wiped sweat off his fur with a large blue handkerchief. "How about over there?"

"Oh, there's a cloud or two over Turtle Pond, but it's hot here too. . . ."

In short, for the rest of the day there were only about fifteen minutes in which they weren't on the phone checking on the weather, comparing meals, making plans for visiting together, and talking about this or that. In the next two weeks they rarely saw each other. Their phone calls sounded pretty much like this:

Buzz . . . buzz . . .

"Hello?"

"Hello."

"Is that you?"

"Yes. Who's that?"

"Me."

"Hi."

"Hi."

"How are ya?"

"Oh . . . okay." Pause. "And you?"

"Fine."

"How's the weather?"

"Fine."

"What's up?"

"Oh . . . not much." Long pause.

"Well . . ."

Loooong pause.

"Why don't you say something?"

"What should I say?"

"Something."

Long pause.

"Come on!"

I don't feel I can say things over the phone, Bear would have liked to say quite often, and sometimes he said it.

Then, one day, a very anxious ring woke Bear up from his third extra morning snooze.

"This is an emergency," Pig squealed, so loud that the phone nearly fell out of Bear's paw. "Come over as fast as you can."

Bear jumped out of bed, grabbed an emergency kit that he'd been collecting with Pig's advice, tossed it on his back, and fell over under the weight. No wonder, for the kit

contained a pick and shovel, a life jacket, seventeen pounds of vitamins, eye drops, bandages, splints, first aid booklets, a blood-pressure meter, a tire gauge, canned apricots, three pounds of chocolate, and a fire extinguisher.

For a while, Bear lay trapped in the emergency-kit straps, moving his legs in the air like a bug turned over on its back. At that moment the phone started ringing again. Bear managed to roll over, and the emergency kit pinned him to the ground. The phone rang on and on, seeming to grow twice as loud with every chime.

It was still ringing when Pig opened the door and freed Bear, who had nearly suffocated under the heavy pack.

"Thank you, thank you," mumbled Bear after Pig helped him to his rocker.

"What's wrong with you?" Pig said. "One doesn't get into an emergency if one has been called to an emergency! And, anyway, why didn't you call me? For once you had a chance to make an emergency call and you botched it. What have we got the phones for?"

"The phone was busy, and I was trapped under a real heavy emergency. Oh, my goodness, my head . . . Could you answer that phone, please? It's been ringing for at least an hour. I hope it's not another emergency."

"Hello," Pig said into the receiver. "Hello? Hello? Hello?

Hello?" He made puzzled grimaces and gestures toward Bear. "Hello? Hello, hello! Hellooo . . . hello? Hallo? Hullo? Hello. Hello? There's no one there," he whispered, covering the receiver clumsily with one hoof. "Hello. . . . Hellooo. . . ."

"Stop it," moaned Bear. "It's worse than the ringing."

"Hello? Oh! I think it's me calling," Pig said.

"What?" Bear jumped up in his chair. "You mean, you are talking to yourself on the phone?"

"I think so."

"Let me hear."

Pig stretched out his hoof with the receiver, but he pulled it back before Bear's paw could reach it. "I mean, it's been me

ringing the phone. I thought you were gone, but I left the phone ringing while I came over here in case you had returned in the meantime."

"I see," Bear said. "That was very thoughtful of you. Now, why did you call me in the first place?"

"Oh, my goodness, you're right! I called you because there was a terrible emergency over in my cottage. Let's get going right now."

"Do I need . . ." Bear waved dizzily toward the enormous pack on the floor.

"No, no," squealed Pig. "Just come with me."

"Is there any danger?" Bear inquired along the way.

"Quite a lot."

"Maybe we should make a circle through the forest to get around to the back door?"

"No need."

"But—"

"No need."

Twenty minutes later, Pig and Bear entered the cottage door. Bear was expecting all kinds of slimy emergencies with big claws to lurch out of the dark corners and jump on his back. He was quite startled when Pig thrust a piece of paper into his paw.

"Here it is."

"What?"

"The emergency."

"What do you mean? It's a piece of paper."

"A horrible piece of paper."

"I don't get it." Bear turned the paper around in his paws.

"Read it!"

"It says 'Tinkerbell . . . Please pay . . .' What is it?"

Pig looked over his shoulder and whispered, "It's a phone bill."

"What's horrible about that?"

"Just look at the bottom."

Bear looked. The number at the bottom was big. Slimy. It had enormous sharp claws. "Oh, my goodness! This *is* an emergency! But it was supposed to be . . . What did you say? Only 7.2 cents, wasn't it?"

"For a short urgent message. That's what the phone is for. Look above that."

"Ten thousand, two hundred and seventy-one." Bear read the numbers one by one. "What's that? A phone number?"

"That's the number of minutes we spent on the phone in the last two weeks. I met a frog while I was going over to your place, and she told me that number means we had been on the phone for over twelve hours a day. She said it wasn't really enough for *The Squirrels' Book of Forest Records*, though."

But neither Pig nor Bear cared about breaking the record set by a pair of blue magpies who stayed on the phone from January till June. From that day on, they used their phones hardly at all, spending more time together than ever before and talking plenty about things that, somehow, they had not been able to say over the phone.